Kenya's Family Reunion

by Juwanda G. Ford
Illustrated by Cristina Ong

SCHOLASTIC INC.

New York   Toronto   London   Auckland   Sydney

ISBN 0-590-53736-9

Kenya is a trademark of Tyco Industries used with permission.
Copyright © 1996 by Tyco Industries, Inc.
All rights reserved. Published by Scholastic Inc.

12 11 10 9 8 7 6 5 4 3 2   6 7 8 9/9 0 1/0

Printed in the U.S.A.   24

First Scholastic printing, May 1996

Kenya woke up with the sun and dressed quickly. She hurried to her parents' bedroom door. She had to make sure they didn't oversleep. Today they were leaving for their annual family reunion.

"It's time to get up!" Kenya shouted.

Her parents were already up and dressed.

"Let's go! Let's go!" Kenya cried.

"Calm down, sweetie," her mother said. "We have to eat breakfast before we go anywhere."

After breakfast, Kenya helped her father get the car ready for the trip. Her mom packed the suitcases in the trunk of the car. Then they were all set to leave.

The family reunion was always held at Kenya's grandfather's farmhouse in the country. Fifty years ago, Grandpa had built the house himself. He named it "The Alpha," which means the beginning.

The drive there was very beautiful. They passed open markets and fields full of wheat and sugarcane.

After driving all day, the family finally arrived at Grandpa's house.

"We're here! We're here!" Kenya shouted as she ran to hug her grandfather.

"What have you been eating to grow so big?" Grandpa said, smiling.

"I've been eating tall pudding and drinking growing juice!" Kenya answered. They both burst into laughter at their private joke.

Soon all the relatives were hugging and kissing hello.
Afterward, Kenya and her young cousins Tyrone, Sarah,
and DJ (short for David, Jr.) ran off to play.

They played their favorite game, hide-and-seek.
They hid in the old tool shed...behind bales of
hay...in the fields....
"Come out, come out wherever you are!" echoed
all over the farm.

From their hiding places, the children soon heard the dinner bell sounding loudly. RRING-A-LING RRING-A-LING!

Sarah popped out from her hiding place. "Time to eat!" she yelled, licking her lips.

"Last one back is a rotten egg!" DJ cried. Then they all raced toward the house.

Uncle Raymond met them as they charged in the back door to the kitchen. "Hold it!" he commanded.

"Uh-oh!" said Kenya. "We forgot to stop at the water pump and wash up."

"That's right," said Uncle Raymond.

So off they went to wash their faces and hands.

When they got back to the house, Kenya's mom and dad were helping Aunt Clarice set out the food and drinks. Everyone gathered around the table and Grandpa said the grace.

"Amen…let's eat!" said cousin Eddie when Grandpa finished.

They passed big bowls of food around the table. There was corn on the cob, mashed potatoes, green beans, and a platter full of barbecue ribs.

Later that evening, everyone except Grandpa gathered for a meeting. Grandpa always went to bed right after dinner. Clarice read through the events planned for the week. "Since this year marks the fiftieth anniversary of this house," she said, "I think we should have a special celebration or something."

"Let's have a party!" DJ yelled.

"We already have a special dinner party planned for Sunday," said his father David, Sr.

"Let's each make something. Let it be a surprise for Grandpa!" Aunt Ruby said. Aunt Ruby was an art teacher. She helped Kenya and her cousins make all kinds of arts-and-crafts during the other reunions.

"But I can't make anything by myself," DJ said sadly.

"I'll help you," Kenya said, taking his hand. She loved playing with DJ because it was like having a little brother.

"Why don't all of you kids make something together," Kenya's father suggested.

The next day, Kenya and her cousins held their own meeting in the old woodshed they used as their playhouse.

"What are we going to make?" DJ asked.

"I have an idea," Kenya exclaimed. And she explained it to them.

"That sounds great!" Sarah nodded. "And we could ask Aunt Ruby to help us!"

The kids found Aunt Ruby on the front porch.

"We need your help with our gift," said Tyrone, catching his breath. "We want to—"

"Wait," Kenya interrupted him. "Let DJ explain it."

DJ could hardly control his excitement as he told Aunt Ruby the plan.

Everyone liked the children's plan so much, they decided to make it their gift, too.

After the sunrise breakfast the next morning,
Grandpa and Kenya's dad loaded the children into
the Jeep and off they went fishing.

While they were gone, some of the grown-ups went into town to buy things they would need for their gift.

Clarice found perfect old lamps, electrical wires, and light fixtures. Maurice bought fence materials. Eddie got sod and flowers.

Later that night, as soon as Grandpa went off to bed, everyone began working on the gift in the playhouse.

The following day was the family picnic. The family ate...they had potato sack races...they played horseshoe...they went swimming in the lake.

Grandpa was having a great time.

"Just wait till he sees our gift!" Clarice said smiling.

By the end of the week, Grandpa still had no idea they were planning a surprise for him. As soon as he left with Uncle Raymond to go pick up the weekly mail, everyone rushed to put the finishing touches on the gift.

Kenya, Tyrone, and Sarah painted the fence and porch furniture. DJ's job was to roll bales of hay.

The final dinner came too soon. No one was ready to say good-bye. The last activity was reading through the names on the family tree. Then it was time to give Grandpa his surprise. Sarah and DJ led the way. Tyrone and Kenya followed.

Grandpa's face beamed with love and pride when they unveiled the gift—a miniature of his farmhouse "The Alpha!"